# Expiration Date:
# NEVER

Also by Stephanie Spinner
and Terry Bisson

## Be First in the Universe

# Expiration Date:
# NEVER

## Stephanie Spinner
### and
## Terry Bisson

DELACORTE PRESS

Published by
Delacorte Press
an imprint of
Random House Children's Books
a division of Random House, Inc.
1540 Broadway
New York, New York 10036

Visit us on the Web! www.randomhouse.com/kids
Educators and librarians, for a variety of teaching tools, visit us at
www.randomhouse.com/teachers

**Library of Congress Cataloging-in-Publication Data**
Spinner, Stephanie.
    Expiration date: never / Stephanie Spinner and Terry Bisson.
        p.   cm.
    Sequel to: Be first in the universe.
    Summary: Their alien friend Gemini Jack tries to help twins Tod and Tessa but
his actions backfire when he turns the evil Gneiss twins super-nice and removes
drummer Nigel Throbber's celebrity by spraying him with permanent Fame Ban.
    ISBN 0-385-32690-4
    1. Twins—Fiction. 2. Extraterrestrial beings—Fiction. 3. Science fiction.]
I. Bisson, Terry. II. Title.
PZ7.S7567 Ex   2001
[Fic]—dc21

                                                                00-045172

The text of this book is set in 13-point Goudy.
Book design by Debora Smith
Manufactured in the United States of America
May 2001
10  9  8  7  6  5  4  3  2  1
BVG

*For Chase and Leighlan,*
*two grand children who love to read*
*—T.B.*

# chapter 1

"Tessa! Hey! Guess who I saw at the mall—"

Tessa Gibson turned. But before she could respond to her twin brother, Tod, who was just getting off his bike, a terrible force struck her from behind and sent her flying.

"Ooooww!" she cried.

"Baaa."

KERWHAP!

She hit the ground so hard that her eyes filled with tears and her mouth filled with dirt. For a second she didn't know what had hit her, and that was scary. Then she did, which was even worse.

Once again she'd been outsmarted—by a goat.

He stood there staring at her without the slightest remorse as she sat up, groaning.

Twist, the most beautiful of her grandfather's

prized Patagonians, was silky-coated, curly-horned, straight-legged, and golden-eyed.

He was also as mean as a snake.

This was the second time in a week he'd butted Tessa. He and his sister, Shout, were showing her no mercy, and Tessa had the black-and-blue marks to prove it.

"You used to be bad. Now you are *evil*," she told him, half-wishing he'd choke on the organic carrot he was chewing. In response he wiggled his goatee.

Tod dropped his bike and hurried over. "My fault," he said. "Sorry." He helped her up.

"It's okay," Tessa mumbled, wiping her eyes quickly.

"You can't turn your back on him," said Tod as Tessa brushed hay and dirt off her shorts and out of her curly reddish hair. "He holds grudges, remember?"

"What's his problem, anyway? I wasn't torturing him, I was just trying to tag him." The twins' grandfather, Lou, planned to show the goats at the Middle County Livestock Fair next week, and they had to be tagged to enter. Every time the twins tossed a coin for the job, Tessa lost.

"You called him Butthead yesterday," Tod reminded her. "Maybe it made him mad."

"He is a butthead. Besides," she added as they

walked to the house, "when did goats start understanding English?"

"These are no ordinary goats," said Tod, doing a pretty fair imitation of their grandfather. Lou tended to be semimystical, especially about his goats. He talked to them and sang to them, and lately he'd started wanting to win blue ribbons with them. Meanwhile, his wife, Lulu, ran an organic dessert business and wrote cookbooks.

Lou and Lulu were old-fashioned hippies. They loved nature, believed in karma, and danced around the kitchen to old rock and roll.

"No joke," said Tessa. "They've gone over to the Dark Side." She had just started reading some of Tod's old *Star Wars* books.

Tod stopped. "That reminds me!" he said. "Guess who I saw at the mall today?"

"Darth Vader?"

"No. Jack!" Tod was usually calm and self-contained, but now there was a note of real excitement in his voice.

"Gemini Jack?" Tessa's eyebrows flew up and her cheeks turned pink. "Really?" Tall, courteous, many-fingered Jack was from a faraway twin planet, but he sometimes managed a store at the mall, which was where Tod and Tessa had met him. They were the only ones who knew he was an alien. Most shoppers assumed he was dressed up for a promotion.

"I thought he was on Gemini, fighting the Vorons," said Tessa as they walked into the kitchen.

"The who?" asked their grandmother Lulu, breaking eggs into a bowl.

Tod and Tessa exchanged a quick glance.

"Aliens from a television show," said Tod, and Lulu smiled absently. The Double L Goat Ranch was surrounded by suburbs, but Lulu and Lou knew next to nothing about television, movies, fast food, or the other essentials of normal life. They lived in a world of their own.

Lulu's smile faded. "Tessa, honey, is that hay in your hair? And why's your face all dirty?" She wiped her hands. "Did those darn goats get you again?"

Tessa nodded.

"Was it Twist?"

Tessa nodded again.

"Come here, honeybun," said Lulu. She hugged Tessa, sat her down on a kitchen stool, and kissed the top of her head. "Are you hurt?" she asked.

"I'm okay," said Tessa, enjoying her grandmother's orange-and-vanilla smell.

"Good," said Lulu. "Because guess what? I have a

nice surprise for you." She pulled a postcard out of her shirt pocket. The card was battered and torn, creased and stained, as if it had been rained on, snowed on, and chewed by a camel. The photo showed a camel market in Mongolia.

"From Mom and Dad!" said Tod and Tessa together. Their parents were traveling around the world on a buying trip for their import-export business.

"HEY, KIDS," said the message, which was written in their father's bouncy uppercase lettering, "WE MISS YOU! LOTS OF DELAYS, SO WON'T BE BACK NEXT MONTH. HOME BY LABOR DAY, IF WE HAVE TO HIRE A CAMEL TO CARRY US! MUCH LOVE—"

"Good news or bad?" asked Lou as he walked in.

"Both," Lulu told him. "Bad news is, Twig and Herbert are stuck in Mongolia. Good news is, we get to keep these two a little longer." She ruffled Tessa's hair, then frowned when she hit straw. "Oh, and Twist butted Tessa again."

"He did?" said Lou, looking dismayed. "That is bad news!"

"I couldn't even get a tag on him," said Tessa.

"They're getting meaner and meaner," said Lulu.

"The livestock show is next week," said Lou. "I'll

tag them myself, and I'll sell them—after I've shown them. It won't be easy . . ." His normally cheerful face looked pained.

Lulu started to say something, then stopped.

"Who would even buy them?" asked Tessa.

"Goat fanciers aren't looking for good manners," said Lou. "They want conformation and bloodlines. Which Twist and Shout have. They're no ordinary goats, you know. They've got a great pedigree." Lou's bushy eyebrows came together like two caterpillars and his eyes turned dreamy, signs that a story was coming.

"An old friend gave them to me . . . ," he began.

"Some friend," said Tessa.

"I'm sorry for what they did to you, Tess," said Lou. "And you're right—I shouldn't keep them if they can't behave."

"Let's put an ad in the paper," said Lulu firmly.

Lou winced. "I did promise Homer I'd let him know if I ever decided to sell them," he said.

"Homer the mandolin player?" asked Lulu. Lou and some friends got together every now and then to play old-timey country music.

"And the manager of Natureland," said Lou.

"Natureland at the mall?" asked the twins.

Lou nodded, with just the hint of a smile. "I could

call him," he said. "Or . . . you could deliver the message in person. Think you're up to it?"

"Yes!" cried Tessa, jumping to her feet.

"Cool," murmured Tod, who was a lot more reserved than his twin.

"Groovy," said Lou. He disappeared for a moment, returning with a photo of himself kneeling between the goats.

"Give this to Homer, okay?" he said. "He can hang it on his bulletin board with my phone number as a reminder."

"Consider it done," said Tod, putting the photo in his pack. He rushed out after Tessa.

"Back by dinnertime!" called Lulu.

"Okay!" called the twins from their bikes.

"Baaa!" called the goats from their pen.

Lulu turned on the radio and got a Beatles song. Lou grinned.

"Let's dance," he said.

# chapter 2

"So tell me more about seeing Jack," said Tessa, as she and Tod approached the mall. "Is he still up on Level Three? Let's go there first."

"Natureland first," said Tod. "Remember?"

"I guess," said Tessa, who had forgotten.

"I'll tell you about Jack on the way," said Tod.

The Middle Valley Mall's huge parking lot swarmed with cars and people. Music was playing, lights flashed on and off, and an enticing smell—part bubble gum, part brand-new plastic—tickled the twins' noses. They parked their bikes and headed for the main entrance.

"Look at that," said Tod as they passed a mountainous SUV painted with a camouflage design, like an army tank, and parked in a no-parking zone. "A Humvee. Wonder who it belongs to."

"Somebody important," said Tessa. "No ordinary person would drive a thing like that."

"Mmm," said Tod, who thought the Hummer looked very cool in a multiple-explosion, action-movie kind of way. He kept this thought to himself, however, and pushed through the revolving doors behind Tessa.

The mall directory told them that Natureland was on Level 2, so they set off for the escalator. Middle Valley Mall was always busy, but today it seemed especially crowded. The throng of shoppers, strollers, mall-walkers and Walkman-wearers was like a dense, slow-moving human obstacle course.

As they approached the escalator, Tessa saw a long line of people snaking around the wishing well. "What's that about?" she wondered aloud.

"Beats me," said Tod.

"Not too hard, I hope, and never with a stick!" said a cheerful voice.

"Oh, hi, Watson," said Tessa politely. Watson was a school guard by day and a mall guard by night, but his dream was to do stand-up comedy. He never stopped practicing. In Tessa's opinion, Watson's jokes sounded as if they had been made up by toddlers giddy on apple juice.

"Hey, Watson! What's up?" exclaimed Tod. Unlike Tessa, he thought Watson was really funny, though he couldn't explain why.

"Balloons. Hemlines. Stock prices," replied Watson. "And celebrity."

"Celebrity?" Tessa waited for the punch line.

Instead Watson pressed his hands together as if in prayer. "A rock star," he said reverently, "in our very own mall. Nigel Throbber."

"Who?"

"*Who?*" the guard echoed. "Only the original drummer with Velvet Trampoline, one of the greatest bands of all time, that's who! V.T. was right up there with Blind Faith and Led Zeppelin!" said Watson. "Platinum records. World tours. Rockumentaries! Nigel's a legend. Or at least he was."

"I think I've heard his name," said Tessa. "Not sure, though . . ."

Tod shrugged.

"Well, you might not get to see him," said Watson, "because lots of people *do* remember him, and the line's about a mile long. Which reminds me— I better go. Promised I'd help with crowd control." He pushed his way back into the throng.

"Bye." Tod pulled Tessa in the direction of the escalator. They had to go slowly, because part of the line blocked their way. And then, just as they were stepping onto the escalator—

"Tod! Tessa!" called a pair of familiar voices. "Wait!"

"Oh, no." Tessa's face fell.

Tod made a quiet choking noise.

Waving hard and beckoning to them from the line were the only other twins at Middle Valley Middle School, Ned and Nancy Gneiss.

The Gneiss twins were mean and sneaky. They had dark impulses. They scared their own mother—or they used to, until, without letting them know about it, Jack the alien extracted some of their evil DNA for use on his own planet.

This highly secret operation, which only Tod and Tessa knew about, had affected the Gneiss twins in a surprising way: It had transformed them. No longer were they nasty, dishonest, and calculating. Now they were helpful, kind, thoughtful, and enthusiastic. Cheery. Sincere. Upbeat. Friendly. Sickeningly, disgustingly . . . nice.

"Hey, you guys!" Ned beamed at them.

"Hey," replied Tod and Tessa with no enthusiasm whatsoever.

"Did you see who's here today?" Nancy asked Tod, standing very close to him and speaking very slowly and softly.

"Let me guess," said Tessa. "Some obscure old rock star?"

"Nigel Throbber's really famous!" said Ned. "Look at this crowd!" He gestured enthusiastically.

"Famous for what?" asked Tod, trying to back away from Nancy.

"Oh, who cares for what?" said Nancy. "A celebrity is somebody who's famous for being famous. You know that, Tod!" She moved a little closer to him.

"And we're practically at the beginning of the line," Ned told them. "Awesome, huh?"

"Totally," said Tod. This sounded like the old Ned, he thought, the one who was happy because he had a place in line and you didn't. I like him better when he gloats, thought Tod. He couldn't stand the Gneiss twins' gooey new friendliness.

"You can have my place," Nancy told Tod, giving him a billion-watt smile.

"Tessa, you can have mine," said Ned. "We're learning to share."

"Especially with you . . . ," Nancy said to Tod, her voice sugary, her eyes wide.

". . . Our best friends," finished Ned.

This is getting way out of hand! thought Tessa. "We like you, too," she said, "but—"

*Beep.* The tiny noise came from Tessa's backpack.

"We'd like to get his autograph," said Tod, "but—"

*Beep.* There it was again.

"What was that?" asked Ned.

"It sounded kind of familiar," said Nancy.

It ought to, thought Tessa. The beeps came from her e-pet, Effie, who fed on lies and beeped when she heard them. She beeped a lot. "Nothing!" Tessa said quickly.

*Beep!*

Jack the alien had given Effie to Tessa just before returning to his twin planets, Gemini. At first Tessa had been overjoyed. But she had come to realize that owning a pet who beeped at lies could cause certain problems.

". . . we have to deliver this picture," Tod finished, flashing the photo of Lou and the goats as if it were a hall pass.

"Next," said a deep voice.

The twins turned. A middle-aged man with long, thinning hair sat at a table piled high with CDs. He wore leather jeans, studded wristbands, and rose-tinted granny glasses, and he was drumming impatiently on the table with his pen.

"Next?" he repeated in the same deep, gravelly voice.

"Go on," said Ned and Nancy. "Take our place!"

The visiting celebrity looked nice enough to Tessa, like somebody her grandparents might know, but she really wanted to get away from the twins.

"We have to get upstairs," she told them.

"Really? Too bad!" said Ned.

"Before you go, Tod," Nancy said, "I have a question for you." She looked up at him from under her eyelashes. "Have you ever been on a study date?"

"Uh, no," blurted Tod, jumping away from her as if she'd poked him with a stick.

"Maybe you and I—" she began.

"Sorry! We're late!" Tessa grabbed her twin's hand and pulled him onto the escalator. Up they went.

"Wait!" called a deep voice from below.

But they were charging up the steps so fast they didn't hear it.

## chapter 3

"This is great! They look spectacular!" Homer was a short, cheerful man with bright eyes and ears that stuck out like handles. As he admired the photo of Twist and Shout, parrots cawed, monkeys hooted, and snakes hissed; the Natureland sound track was in jungle mode. Something sweet and spicy in the air, an exotic perfume, made Tessa think of big, colorful flowers.

"And they're really for sale?" Homer asked eagerly.

The twins nodded.

"Did Lou say how much he wanted for them?"

"Cheap!" said Tessa. "Ouch!" She glared at Tod, who had kicked her.

"If you call him," said Tod, "he'll tell you all about them."

"Tell me about them? They're beautiful! Two of the finest Patagonians I've ever seen," said Homer. "That's all I need to know—and the price."

"They like to butt people," said Tessa.

"Well, they're goats!" said Homer dismissively.

"They got me twice this week," said Tessa, but her warning about the goats' true nature didn't register with Homer. He was staring past her with a strange expression on his face.

At first Tessa thought she'd upset him, but then she realized he was looking at somebody who'd just come into the store.

"That picture," said a deep voice. Tessa and Tod turned and found themselves facing a man in rose-colored glasses and leather jeans: Nigel Throbber.

"Have a look?" he asked, indicating the photograph.

"Sure," said Homer, handing him the photograph. "Absolutely."

"They're mean," said Tessa.

"But they are pedigreed," added Tod.

Nigel stared at the photo through his rose-colored lenses. "You selling them?" he asked.

"Our grandfather is," said Tod. "He raises goats."

"Hmm. This him, then?" Nigel pointed to Lou, and the twins nodded.

"Fancy that," said Nigel.

"Are you a goat fancier?" asked Tessa. "I mean, do you like goats?"

Nigel smiled. "I like that old goat in the middle," he said.

"That's our grandfather!" said Tod, surprised at Nigel's rudeness.

Nigel grinned, raising his hands. "Just kidding. Actually hoping to—"

Before he could finish his sentence, the Natureland sound track changed and an uneven murmur drowned out the monkeys and the birds and the snakes.

A waterfall? wondered Tessa.

A river? wondered Tod.

"Blast!" said Nigel, whirling toward the door. "They found me."

Tod and Tessa turned also. The source of the waterfall sound was a small crowd, rushing down the corridor toward the store. One or two people started knocking on the door, which seemed to be locked.

"Saw you, saw the photo, followed you up here," said Nigel. "But the fans won't have it, will they?" He sighed. "Fame," he said. "Bit of a drag, quite honestly."[1]

---

[1]Celebrity Rule #1: Celebrities always say they hate being famous.

*Beep!* The noise came from Tessa's pack, but Nigel ignored it. "Know another way out of here?" he asked.

"We can get you to the escalator," said Tod.

"First we have to get out of the store," said Tessa. The crowd now blocked the front of the store, and eager faces were peering through the windows. A few people were waving hopefully.

Homer, who had been too overcome in Nigel's presence to say a word until now, gasped something that sounded like "Follow me." He led them to a rear exit, where he paused.

Before unlocking the door, he handed Nigel a pen and a piece of paper.

What's he doing? wondered the twins.

Nigel knew.

He scrawled his name. Then Homer, flushing with pleasure, let them out.

## chapter 4

**N**igel stopped in his tracks. "Blast," he said again. The escalator was crowded with people, some climbing up, others looking around eagerly, and then—

"There he is!"

"Nigel!"

"*Nige!* Hey, man!"

The twins realized they were with somebody who was actually being chased by a crowd. It was exciting and a little scary, like a weird mutant version of hide-and-seek.

"Let's go up instead of down," said Tod.

"Good idea," said Tessa.

She wheeled, Tod and Nigel followed, and then they were at the other end of the corridor, on the Up escalator.

"Hate being chased," muttered Nigel.

*Beep beep.*

Tessa ignored Effie. The sound of the crowd made her jittery—so jittery that she scrambled up the moving staircase, pulling Tod with her. "Hurry!" she called to Nigel, who was lagging behind.

When they were on Level 3 she whirled, and Tod turned with her as if they were playing Snap the Whip.

And that was when it happened.

The twins saw red—a neon flash that came and went so quickly it might have been a hallucination.

They froze and looked at each other. Then they took a slow, deliberate step backward, in unison.

This time they saw it more clearly.

"Holy moly!" A big smile broke out on Tessa's face when she saw the red neon sign.

## GEMINI JACK'S U RENT ALL
### Be First in the Universe!

It flashed on, then off.

"Whoa," said Tod. "I forgot Jack's store is on Level Three."

"But that's great!" cried Tessa. "He'll hide us!"

"Jack doesn't want us bringing in strangers," said Tod.

"Nigel's not a stranger, he's a celebrity,"[2] said Tessa.

"Jack? Who's Jack?" asked Nigel, who was not used to people talking about anybody but Nigel.

"A friend," said Tessa. She and Tod smiled at each other.

"That's cool," said Nigel.

You don't know how cool, thought Tessa, pushing the door open.

*Bong!* The sound, halfway between a chime and a gong, hummed in their ears as they walked inside.

And there he was, behind the counter—Jack the alien from the twin planets of Gemini. As always, his dark eyes glittered, and his mouth only appeared when he talked.

"Tod! Tessa! Just the humans I wanted to see," said Jack. "How are you? And how is my little Fib Muncher?" he added, referring to Effie.

"She's fine," said Tessa, who was very attached to Effie. "She, uh, misses you, of course."

*Beep beep!* came from Tessa's pack.

Jack smiled a sad smile. "I didn't think she would miss me," he said.

*Beep beep.*

Time to change the subject, thought Tessa. "What

---

[1]Celebrity Rule #2: Celebrities are exempt from the usual rules.

are you doing here?" she asked Jack. "We thought you'd gone back to Gemin—"

Tod elbowed her, rolling his eyes in Nigel's direction.

"What about him?" asked Tessa.

"He can't know about Jack," Tod said quietly. "That he's, uh, not from here."

"Like he cares?" responded Tessa.

She had a point. Tod saw that Nigel's attention wasn't on Jack but on his own colorful reflection in the store window.[3]

"I'll explain tomorrow," said Jack, with a glance at Nigel. "Can you return then?" he asked.

"Definitely," said Tod. Maybe Jack's got some gadget that will make Nancy hate me! he thought. "Definitely!" he repeated.

"Sure," said Tessa. "But first we have to get this guy out of here. He's famous, and there's a crowd chasing him."

"I think I can help you," said Jack. He reached under the counter and pulled out a spray can. "This is very popular in some parts of the galaxy," he said.

"Wait a second. There are celebrities in outer space?" asked Tessa.

---

[3]Celebrity Rule #3: Celebrities are mainly interested in themselves.

"They're everywhere," said Jack. "And when they want relief from being famous, they use Fame Ban."

At the word *fame*, Nigel was at their side. "Fame what?" he asked, looking at the can.

"Fame Ban," said Jack. "Just spray a little on your hands and face and you'll go unrecognized."

Nigel looked doubtful. "How long does it last?" he asked.

"About fifteen Earth min . . . ah . . . about fifteen minutes," said Jack.

"Fifteen minutes of nonfame? Perfect!" Nigel grabbed the can and sprayed himself.

"Smells like deodorant," said Tessa.

"Deodor what?" asked Jack.

Nigel peered at Jack through his rose-colored spectacles. "Hey, man, good one," he snorted, raising a massive hand for a high five.

Jack's mouth disappeared as he tried to make sense of Nigel's response. He raised one of his many-fingered hands.

Before Nigel could hit it, Tod said, "If you want to talk about the goats, we'd better go. I think I hear the crowd."

*Beep*, said Effie.

"See you tomorrow," said Jack.

The twins left the store bracing themselves for

Nigel's fans, but the hallway was quiet, and the few shoppers ambling along showed absolutely no interest in him.

Nigel stood there, looking almost disappointed. Then he snapped his fingers.

"Fame Ban!" he said to the twins, slapping the thighs of his leather jeans. "It works! What a relief!"

*Beep beep!* said Effie.

# chapter 5

Nobody even glanced at them as they made their way down to Level 1, where Tod saw that the clock in the window of Home Office Depot said 6:10.

He groaned. "We're late," he said. "We'd better hurry." Lou and Lulu were strict about punctuality, especially when the twins were due home from the mall.

"Why?" asked Nigel.

"Our grandparents will worry," said Tod.

"They hate the mall," said Tessa as they left the building.

"Give you a ride home," said Nigel. "Got my wheels right here."

"We're not supposed to ride with strangers," said Tessa.

"He's not a stranger, he's a celebrity,"[4] replied Tod, seeing the big, camouflage-painted Humvee near the entrance and realizing it was Nigel's. "You said so yourself."

"*Was* a celebrity," corrected Nigel, jokingly, "thanks to Fame Ban." He looked around, but nobody recognized him, though many people stared at the Humvee.

"We rode our bikes here," said Tod.

"Oh! Right," said Tessa.

"Stick 'em in back," said Nigel. "They'll fit." He opened the doors with a remote control. "See?" The rear compartment was carpeted, and big enough for half a dozen bikes.

"Okay!" The twins got their bikes and Nigel loaded them in. For such an old guy he had very muscular arms, Tod noticed.

"Let's rock and roll!" he said, when they had all fastened their seatbelts. Tod felt a tingle of anticipation. The Humvee's seats were leather and very soft. The dashboard had more dials and gauges than a fighter jet. And the instant Nigel turned the ignition key, the sound system exploded around them, blasting drum music so loud that Tessa clapped her hands over her ears.

---

[4]Celebrity Rule #4: See Celebrity Rule #2.

Nigel took off. "Tell me where," he shouted, beating time on the steering wheel.

Tod used sign language to direct Nigel and they were at the ranch in five minutes. As they pulled into the driveway, Lou and Lulu appeared on the porch.

Uh-oh, thought the twins.

Nigel turned off the sound. The twins jumped out of the Humvee.

"You're late," said Lou and Lulu, frowning.

Then their frowns disappeared. They stepped off the porch.

"Nigel?" they said.

"Lou!" cried Nigel. "Lulu!"

# *chapter 6*

"**M**om!"

Ned and Nancy burst into their house, greeting Mrs. Gneiss as if they hadn't seen her in years.

They've only been gone for two hours, she thought as the twins took turns kissing her hello. Why are they making such a fuss?

Mrs. Gneiss still wasn't used to the way her children were behaving these days. All the hugging and kissing, the compliments and gifts, made her just a little uncomfortable. And the tiniest bit guilty—because she knew she should be happier about the way they'd changed. They used to be so bad-tempered and nasty that she worried about them all the time. Now they were so nice that she had no reason to worry about them.

But she did.

She took the shopping bag Nancy handed her and pretended to be pleased, even though she was really only puzzled. Why in heaven's name were her children giving her a CD called *Drums on the Danube* by somebody named Nigel Throbber?

"This looks . . . interesting," she said.

"He signed it, Mom," said Nancy. "Look." She pointed to the jagged purple signature that zigzagged across the package.

"He's really famous," said Ned. "We waited in line for him and everything."

"Plus, there's a live concert in Romania on it," said Nancy. "In Bucharest. Isn't that where our family came from?"

"Some of them," said Mrs. Gneiss a little blankly. The twins had developed a burning interest in their ethnic heritage lately. They were even talking about taking a Romanian folk-dancing class, something that would have drawn hisses of contempt a few months ago—if anyone had dared suggest it.

"Do you like it, Mom?" asked Nancy, who never used to care what her mother thought or felt about anything.

"I do," said Mrs. Gneiss. "I do. It's a very nice gift.

So thoughtful of you." Suddenly she felt very tired. "I think I'll start reading the liner notes right now," she said, backing up the stairs.

"We love you, Mother," intoned her children as she made her escape.

# chapter 7

"**N**igel!"

"Lou! Lulu!"

Tod and Tessa watched, amazed, as Nigel Throbber grabbed their grandparents in a bear hug. Then they all jumped off the porch and did a silly little dance together on the grass.

"You know each other?" asked Tessa when her grandmother stopped to catch her breath.

"We certainly do," said Lulu. "Nigel introduced us."

"I thought you and Grandpa met at Woodstock," said Tod.

"We did," said Lou, panting.

"Just before my first set," said Nigel.

"You didn't tell us you knew them!" Tessa said to Nigel.

"Did you recognize Lou from the photo?" asked Tod.

Nigel nodded. "My little surprise," he confessed with a lopsided smile. "Couldn't resist."

"Come on inside, man!" said Lou, slapping Nigel on the back. "This is great!"

"Crikey! What's that smell?" asked Nigel when they were all in the kitchen.

"Just some brownies," said Lulu. She gave him one and he ate it in two bites.

"*Ow!*" he yelped appreciatively. "Baker goddess!" He did a drumroll on the table with his fingers.

Lulu smiled modestly.

"Even back then," he said to the twins. "Lulu's cookies? Made grown men weep."

"At Woodstock?" asked Tod.

"Sure at Woodstock," said Nigel. "Absolutely at Woodstock! She was there with Wild Oats—"

"—the commune," explained Lulu. "We were feeding the bands."

"—they flipped for her cookies! Her cookies were the inspiration for 'Purple Haze.'" Nigel looked at the twins. "Jimi himself told me. Not many people know that."

"Wow," said Tessa.

"Cool," said Tod, who had always assumed his

grandparents were exaggerating when they told stories about their hippie days.

"We stayed in touch through the seventies," said Lou.

"Came to my concerts," said Nigel, "then came backstage. Always had some mind-blowing dessert. Still remember that chocolate cake you gave me. What was it called?"

"Nirvana Cake?" Lulu shook her head.

Nigel snapped his fingers and beat out a rapid tattoo on the table. "Nirvana Cake! That's the one!"

Lulu shook her head. "I don't make it anymore— too rich," she said. "One of my nicest customers had a heart attack after he ate one, and I still blame myself. He recovered, but still . . . I should have put a warning label on it."

There was a brief silence.

"Well, hey, man," Lou finally said to Nigel. "It's really great to see you. How'd you find us? We lead a pretty retiring life."

Nigel told Lou and Lulu about following the twins to the pet store, and how they'd dodged the crowd.

"Great kids you got here," he said. "Knew a bloke who helped us right away. Sprayed me with this stuff called Fame Ban. Like invisibility spray. And it worked!"

Lou and Lulu looked at the twins. "Like *what?*" they asked.

"Nothing, really," said Tod quickly.

*Beep beep*, said Effie from inside Tessa's pack.

"It all had to do with the goats," said Tessa hastily. "We had the picture, remember?"

"Nigel saw the picture of you with Twist and Shout," said Tod.

"Far out! You're not interested in Patagonians, are you?" asked Lou.

"Not really," said Nigel. "Met some before, though. Mick fancies them. Claims they only like high profilers."[5]

"High profilers?" Lulu raised an eyebrow.

"You mean celebrities?" asked Lou.

"Mick?" said Tod. "You mean Mick—"

"Of course, sweetie," said Lulu. "Let Nigel finish."

"That's it," said Nigel. "His were pretty well-behaved, but then . . ." Instead of finishing the sentence, he flipped a teaspoon into the air, caught it, grabbed a knife, and beat a rapid tattoo on the kitchen table, ending with a flourish.

Whoa! thought Tessa, who tended to drop things if she wasn't careful.

---

[5] Celebrity Rule #5: Celebrities never refer to themselves as celebrities.

"Want to meet them?" asked Lou.

"They're mean as snakes," warned Lulu.

Meaner, thought Tod.

"Snakes are nicer," said Tessa.

"Why not?" said Nigel. "Might be fun." He jumped up.

"Then let's go," said Lou. "This way." They left by the back door and took the path out to the barn.

"You kids keep your distance," Lou told the twins.

"Fine with me," said Tessa.

"Me too," said Tod. They dropped back, watching as the grown-ups opened the barn doors and slipped inside.

"Wonder why Jack wants to talk to us," whispered Tessa. "Did he tell you when you first saw him?"

"No, I saw him from a distance. But we'll find out tomorrow," said Tod.

The lights in the barn came on. Then they heard Lulu say, "Take it easy with them, Nigel."

Tessa's eyebrows went up. "They hate it when you wake them up," she said to Tod.

"They hate it when *you* wake them up," said Tod. "Because you're not famous."

"Well, excuuuuse me," said Tessa, fighting the urge to stick her tongue out at her brother.

"Please allow me to introduce myself," sang Nigel.

There was a hoarse, surprised shout from Lou.

"Baaa! *Baaa! BAAAA!*" The loud, furiously angry bleating didn't stop when Lulu screamed.

Then Nigel, a human projectile in leather jeans, came flying through the open barn door, limbs flailing, mouth open in surprise. For a few long seconds he was airborne. Until . . . *whomp!* He landed on the ground a few yards from the twins.

"*BAAA!*" went the goats.

"Guess the Fame Ban hasn't worn off yet," whispered Tod.

# chapter 8

*T*hanks to Nigel, the twins got to stay up very late. After his "accident" he hobbled back to the kitchen, where Lulu restored his good humor with half a tray of brownies and some strong coffee.

Then he agreed to stay for dinner, which took longer than usual for Lulu to prepare because she wanted to cook something special. While she worked on a Honk If You Love Cheese pie, Nigel entertained her by drumming on every pot and pan in the kitchen, and by the time they sat down to eat, it was eight-thirty.

After dinner Nigel tried calling a few people on his cell phone. He couldn't reach anybody, so he agreed to stay at the ranch overnight, and then he and Lou and Lulu sat around for a long time talking. It was almost ten before Lou and Lulu remembered that the twins had school the next day and hustled them upstairs.

As she lay in bed with her eyes closed, Tessa heard Nigel talking quietly for a long time. Every now and then her grandparents would respond sympathetically, as if they were trying to cheer him up.

What's he got to be sad about? she wondered, and then she fell asleep.

When the twins met in the cafeteria on Monday, they were both yawning. "Think Nigel's still at the ranch?" asked Tessa.

"Maybe," said Tod. "He was pretty sore last night. Those goats really surprised him."

"They sure did," said Tessa. "I guess they don't care that he's famous."

"Who's famous?" asked Tod's friend Phil.

"Nobody," said Tod, kicking Tessa. They had promised their grandparents not to tell anybody that Nigel was at the ranch.

*Beep beep,* said Effie, who was always happy to have a fib to munch on, even a small one.

Tessa saw her friend Calista and waved. "Let's go," Tod said to Phil. He liked to eat with his own friends. Girls—especially these days—made him nervous.

"Maybe we'll sit with you," said Tessa. A look of

alarm passed over her brother's face. "Just teasing," she said. "See you later." And she headed off in Calista's direction.

Tod's table was rowdy, but he ate quietly, thinking about Jack and his startling reappearance at the mall. Why did the alien want to see Tod and Tessa? Were his planets in trouble again? And what excellent new gadgets was he carrying in his store? Maybe he had some Annoying Girl Repellent. Spray would be fine, thought Tod, or roll-on. Even a pill would be okay. He chewed his organic peanut butter and honey sandwich (a Lulu special) and allowed himself to dream.

Tessa was at his locker after last period. "I'm skipping library," she said. "I want to get to the mall and see what Jack wants."

"Me too," said Tod. "I've been wondering about it all day."

One of Tessa's eyebrows went up and she started to smile. "Aren't you forgetting something?" she asked.

"Like what?"

"Like your study date?"

"My what?"

"Hi, Tod," said a sugary voice. "Where do you want to study?"

Tessa struggled to keep her face expressionless, but it wasn't easy. Nancy Gneiss, once so mean that she wouldn't even look at Tod, was staring at him now with melting adoration.

The tips of Tod's ears turned bright red. His face, on the other hand, became extremely pale. "I, uh, I can't," he stammered. "I have to, uh . . ."

*Beep beep*, said Effie, from Tessa's pack.

Tessa took pity on her twin. "Family emergency," she told Nancy. "We have to run."

*BEEP!*

"Oooh!" said Nancy. "I'm so disappointed!" She looked deep into Tod's eyes, which made him blink rapidly. His face had turned a peculiar white-green color that Tessa thought of as "pre-vomit."

"I had so many things I wanted to ask you," Nancy said to him.

"Some other time," said Tod, backing away.

*Beep beep*, commented Effie.

"What are you grinning about?" Tod snapped to Tessa as they got on their bikes and set off for the mall. Now that they were outside, he looked a lot better.

"Hey! Quit snarling," said Tessa. "You should thank me for saving your life. I got you away from her, didn't I?"

Tod sighed. "Yup. Thanks." They pedaled in silence for a few minutes. "Why is she after me?" he asked after a while. "What does she want?"

"You really don't know?" said Tessa. "It's so obvious."

"Well, then, tell me," said Tod.

"She wants you to carry her books. And sit with her at lunch. And send her notes with big hearts on them. . . ."

"Stop!" Tod howled and covered his ears, nearly falling off his bike. "I don't want to hear any more!"

"He really doesn't," Tessa whispered to Effie, who didn't even think about beeping.

The mall was crowded. Tessa breathed deeply, enjoying the scented air, the soft music, and the sparkly lights. As always, she was happy to be back in the mall's special artificial atmosphere. But her enjoyment didn't last long. She and Tod had barely passed through the revolving doors when they found themselves face to face with Watson.

Tessa got ready to hear a bad joke, which was Watson's customary way of saying hello. Instead he asked, "Have you two seen Ned Gneiss?"

"No," said Tod.

Tessa waited for the punch line. Instead, Watson

rolled his eyes with relief and said, "Good! That kid is driving me nuts."

"He is?" said Tessa. "I thought he and Nancy were behaving especially *nicely* these days. Get it, Watson?"

"Mmm." Watson smiled with an effort. "That's the problem," he said. "These days they're too nice—"

"Really," said Tod.

"—and I can't get used to it. Remember how Ned used to heckle me?"

The twins nodded. "Well, now he's decided I'm a comic genius," said the guard. "He keeps following me around, telling me he's got this great idea—"

"When pigs fly," commented Tessa.

"What is it?" asked Tod.

"A combination comedy club–shish kebab restaurant, and I'll be the featured act. He laughs at all my jokes—"

"He *does?*" As soon as she said it, Tessa was sorry, because Watson's face fell.

"I mean, of course he laughs," she said. "Your jokes are funny."

*Beep beep,* said Effie.

"And you're totally right about Ned," Tessa added. "He and Nancy are definitely acting weird. Something strange has happened to them."

"Maybe they got kidnapped by aliens," suggested Tod.

"Tod!" Tessa said sharply, yanking her brother's arm. "Let's go."

"Where are you off to in such a hurry?" asked Watson.

"Nowhere," said Tessa.

*Beep beep*, said Effie.

"We're going to communicate with alien beings," said Tod as they started up the escalator.

"Very funny," said Watson.

"Yeah, Tod, very funny!" said Tessa as soon as they were out of earshot. "What are you trying to do, tell the whole world about Jack?"

"Relax," said Tod. "When the truth is this weird, nobody believes it. Not even Watson."

# chapter 9

"Tod! Tessa! It is good to see you." Jack's dark eyes gleamed as he welcomed the twins into his store.

"Great to see you, too," said Tessa.

"Yeah," agreed Tod. "Really."

They all smiled. Then Tod said, "So, what's up, Jack? You said you had something to tell us."

"Actually, I've come back to ask you a favor," said Jack.

"A favor?"

"I know it is only a short time since you helped us against the Vorons," said Jack, referring to the aggressive aliens who had been threatening his twin planets, Gemini. "And we are deeply grateful."

"We didn't do much," said Tod. "Just introduced you to the Gneiss twins. Their DNA did the rest."

"You were the one who figured out how to use it

against the Vorons," said Tessa, "not us. That's what saved Gemini."

Jack's eyes dulled a little and his skin lost some of its sheen. He said nothing. Tessa felt a little prickle of worry.

"You *did* save your planets, didn't you?" she asked.

"Well. Not exactly," said Jack. Then he was silent for so long that Tessa's worry turned to alarm. When he was unhappy, Jack's eyes turned gray and stony and his skin took on the pallor of a deep-sea creature unaccustomed to light. That was the way he looked now.

"You mean they invaded anyway?" asked Tod.

Jack nodded. "They just kept coming," he said, "more and more of them."

"On battle cruisers?" asked Tod, feeling a thrill in spite of himself. Interplanetary war was exciting!

"Giant cruisers," said Jack. "Filled with them. It's been horrible! Like the onslaught of a terrible illness! I . . . I was hoping you might help us further," he concluded.

"But the Gneiss twins' DNA is powerful stuff," said Tod. "Wasn't it strong enough to kill the Vorons?"

"Kill?" Jack's mouth shrank to a tiny zero of surprise. "We could never kill them," he said. "Geminis don't kill. Violence is outside our behavioral range."

"Then what . . . ?" Tod was thoroughly puzzled.

"The DNA enables us to be rude to them," said Jack. "We ignore them, or pretend we don't understand when they speak to us in our language. We always give them bad service, sometimes even wrong directions—"

"Wait a minute," said Tessa. "That's your idea of fighting back? Being impolite?"

"*Very* impolite," said Jack. "But it doesn't work! They like it. They find it . . . appealing! Amusing! It may amuse the Vorons," he added, "but it is catastrophic for us. At first there was just a trickle—a package tour or two. Now hordes of them are showing up, vacationing all over Gemini—"

"Vacationing?" said Tessa. "You mean the Vorons are *tourists?*"

"Yes!"

"You called them invaders," Tod pointed out.

"They might as well be," said Jack. "They are loud, clumsy, and stupid. They expect twenty-four-hour room service. And the more we insult them, the more they like it."

"Why can't you just tell them to leave?" asked Tessa.

"We've tried," said Jack. "They laugh at us."

The twins exchanged a look. "Let me get this

straight," said Tod. "They're not waging war on you, they're just hanging around?"

"It is gruesome," said Jack. "Jill and I thought the best place to find a solution was here."

"On Earth? Why?" asked the twins.

Jack hesitated. Tessa realized it was because he didn't want to hurt their feelings.

"You already told us Earth was the most violent place in the universe," said Tod.

Jack's mouth disappeared for a moment. "It's also . . . the most . . . the most . . ."

"The most what?" asked the twins. They would soon wish they hadn't.

# chapter 10

"**A**nnoying?" said Tod a few minutes later as he and Tessa were biking home from the mall. "Can you believe Jack said humans are *annoying?*"

Tessa only pedaled faster. She didn't want to admit it to Tod, but she felt hurt by Jack's assessment of the human race.

How embarrassing to be told that everybody in the universe had such a low opinion of humans! It was like finding out that your entire species had bad breath.

I need some quiet time, she thought.

But that was not to be.

As they approached the house, the twins heard a series of loud noises—clangs, thuds, booms, and bangs.

"What's going on?" shouted Tod as he caught up to her.

Tessa shrugged and shook her head. It was pointless to try to speak over the din.

Lou appeared in the front yard, pushing his rickety old lawn mower. Lulu always teased Lou about his mower, which rattled and squeaked whenever he used it, as if it were complaining.

"It's a-kvetchin'," she liked to say. Today it didn't make a sound—or it least it didn't make a sound that the twins could hear over all the other noise.

"What's happening?" asked Tod, but Lou just waved at them halfheartedly and kept mowing. There was a strange, tense expression on his face—as if he was trying very hard to concentrate. But on what? Tessa wondered.

They walked into the kitchen, which smelled like almonds and vanilla. The noise stopped suddenly when the door closed behind them; it had been coming from the barn.

"Where in the world have you two been?" asked Lulu, setting down a platter of cookies. As usual, she said *world* as if it were some far-flung, exotic place.

"At the mall, buying—uh, school stuff," said Tod.

*Beep beep*, said Effie.

"Just out and around," said Tessa. She had begun to worry about Effie a little. The e-pet fed on lies, and she was hearing an awful lot of them lately. If she heard too many, would she get fat? Explode?

*BOOM! BA BOOM BOOM! BA BOOM CHICKA BLAM!* The noise started up again, louder than ever.

"What *is* that racket?" asked Tod through a mouthful of milk and cookies.

"Racket?" asked Lulu, as if she couldn't hear the crashing din from the barn.

"Yes! Racket!" yelled Tessa, reaching for another cookie.

"Oh, that," said Lulu, and now Tessa saw that her expression was tense, almost closed down, the way Lou's had been. "That's Nigel. He's practicing."

"Where'd he get drums?" asked Tod.

"He keeps a spare set in his Humvee," said Lulu. "And he added some stuff from the barn—buckets and milk pails and old car parts."

*CRASH! BLAM!*

"Isn't it driving you crazy?" asked Tod.

"You're always telling *us* to keep the racket down." Tessa only dared to say this because she knew Lulu couldn't hear her.

"Oh, not at all," said Lulu.

*Beep beep*, said Effie.

Tessa's eyes widened in shock. Lulu was fibbing!

"He's a serious musician, you know," said Lulu. "This piece took him five years to write. And nobody wants to listen to it."

*BOOMBOOMBOOMBOOMBONGGGG!*

"Gee," said Tessa. "Wonder why."

"He's never recorded it or even performed it in public," Lulu went on. "It's kind of sad."

The twins looked at each other.

Sad for who? thought Tod.

Sad for whom? thought Tessa, whose grammar was better than her twin's.

Lulu arranged cream, bowls, and an electric mixer on the counter. "Do your chores, guys," she said. "And be careful."

# *chapter 11*

"**Y**ou go first," said Tessa. She said this every evening when she and Tod set out to feed Twist and Shout, and his response was always the same.

"You," he replied. They compromised by walking into the barn together.

Surprisingly, the goats were at the far end of the barn, huddled against the wall with their heads down. Gone was the evil fury that so often blazed from their eyes; gone was the implacable insolence of their expressions, which always managed to frighten the twins more than they would admit.

Today they just looked miserable.

*Boom de boom boom BOOM! Boom de BOOM!*

Nigel sat in the hayloft, banging away at a collection of drums and old farm equipment with his eyes closed.

"Hi!" called Tessa.

He kept playing as if he hadn't heard her.

As she helped Tod fill the goats' bowls with Purina Goat Chow, Tessa wondered if celebrities had their own kind of etiquette that allowed them to ignore people whenever they wanted to.[6] Maybe so, she thought.

Then Nigel stopped playing, and the rattle of goat food hitting goat dishes was suddenly very loud.

*Deedle de da da da.* He was dialing his cell phone. *Deedle de da da da.* He redialed. Tessa was thinking that the soft little electronic tones were soothing— no, almost beautiful—after all that drumming, when she heard another sound: *click click click click, click click click click.* Two sets of hard little goat hooves were galloping across the barn floor.

Twist and Shout were on the attack.

"Oh, no!" Tessa cried, scrambling for the door. She and Tod got out just ahead of the goats. As they leaned against the closed door, panting, it shook, then shook again. Twist and Shout were butting it from the other side.

"Holy moly!" said Tessa. "We—" But her voice was drowned out by a noise from inside the barn. *Boom da BOOM ca-RASH!* Nigel was practicing again.

⁶Celebrity Rule #6: See Celebrity Rule #2.

Tod peered through a crack in the door, and his eyebrows went up.

"What?" asked Tessa.

He motioned for her to look inside.

Twist and Shout were back at the far end of the barn, huddling against the wall. Once again they looked as if they were trying to escape the sound of Nigel's drumming, which got louder and louder and faster and faster. Once again the goats looked miserable.

"I can't believe I'm saying this," said Tessa, "but I actually feel sorry for them."

Dinner was at six, as always. And as always, they held hands and said grace before eating. Nigel, who came to the table looking grumpy and frustrated, said very little during the meal and didn't twirl his fork once.

For dessert Lulu served strawberry pie with fresh whipped cream. Delectable as it was, it didn't cheer Nigel up. After taking a few bites, he said, "What time is it?" without bothering to look at his watch—a gigantic metal device bristling with dials and buttons.[7]

"Six-forty-five," said Lou.

[7] Celebrity Rule #7: Celebrities always wear fancy watches but never look at them.

"Good—three-forty-five in L.A.," said Nigel. "Time to call my agent." He pulled his phone out and speed-dialed. *Deedle de da da da.*

"Nigel here," he said, then frowned at the response he got. "Throbber," he said edgily. There was a pause.

"What do you *mean* he's in a meeting?" exclaimed Nigel. "He's been in a meeting for two bloody days now! Tell him it's *Nigel*. Nigel *Throbber!*"[8]

Lou offered Nigel more pie. Nigel shook his head, listening intently to the voice on the phone. Then he slammed it onto the table. "They put me on hold!" he said. "Unbelievable!"[9]

"How was school today, guys?" asked Lou.

"Fascinating," said Tod.

*Beep beep*, said Effie.

"What was that?" asked Lulu.

"Nothing," said Tod, trying to help Tessa out.

*Beep BEEP*, said Effie.

"Young lady!" said Lulu sternly. "Electronic devices don't belong at the dinner table."

"Whoops! Sorry," said Tessa, quickly jumping up to put her backpack on the stairway. As she sat down at

---

[8] Celebrity Rule #8: Celebrities think their names are magic if said loudly enough.

[9] Celebrity Rule #9: Celebrities are never put on hold.

the table again, a tinny little sound—recorded music—came from Nigel's cell phone. He was still on hold.

They all looked at him. He looked back. Then, finally, he clicked the phone shut. "I'll try later," he said. "Don't care, anyway."

*Beep beep*, called Effie.

# chapter 12

**B**reakfast was usually a cheery time at the ranch, but this morning it was like a meeting of newly risen zombies. Tod and Tessa yawned and mumbled. Lou, who often hummed old rock songs while he squeezed orange juice, hardly made a sound. Lulu stirred the cinnamon oatmeal on the stove in slow motion, eyes bleary.

As for Nigel, the bags under his eyes were duffel-size.

"You kids sleep all right?" asked Lou.

"Mmm," said Tod noncommittally. He'd had some strange dreams—maybe because of Nigel's drumming—but he wasn't about to mention them.

"Mmm," echoed Tessa. She'd had weird dreams also, but that was nothing new. She and Tod often had similar dreams, something they'd discovered when they were younger. They'd learned that there was less fuss if they kept quiet about it.

"Nigel was up pretty late playing the drums," said Lulu, yawning.

"Got to get the second movement perfect," said Nigel. "Didn't disturb anyone, did I?"

"Oh, no," said Lulu.

"Nope," said Lou, rubbing his eyes.

*Beep beep*, said Effie.

The twins' eyes met. Their grandparents were lying!

"Great to have a chance to work on the piece," said Nigel. "Usually too busy. And most hotels don't allow drumming at night."

"Imagine that," drawled Lulu, serving up the oatmeal.

"Hmm," said Lou, and then yawned so hugely that Tessa could see his tonsils.

Nigel dipped his spoon in his oatmeal but didn't eat, just looked down at his bowl. "Truth is," he said, "you're the only people who'll even let me play it. My agents hate it. Record company won't release it. Manager won't let me perform it in public."

Nigel's voice was so deep and sad that everybody stared at him. "Nearly come to blows over it," he confessed.

"Maybe folks don't want to sit through long drum solos anymore," said Lulu.

"Maybe the public's not ready," said Lou.

"What my agents say," agreed Nigel. "But how do people know they don't like it if they can't even hear it?"

"There's no accountin' for taste, Nigel," said Lulu consolingly.

"What I say to my agents," said Nigel. "Gave 'em an ultimatum. Book me playing the Drummerdämmerung—wherever, whenever—or I quit." He pulled out his cell phone and looked at it gloomily. "Maybe it's my phone," he said uncertainly.

"But what about your tour?" asked Lou.

"And your concert schedule?" asked Lulu.

Nigel shrugged. "Don't care about 'em," he said. "Need a break. Got to do some soul-searching. Figure out what to do next." For once his hands were still.

Lou and Lulu's eyes met. "Hey, man, stay with us," said Lou. "Hang at the ranch while you think things through. Might do you some good."

"Stay as long as you like," said Lulu.

"Our *casa* is *su casa*," said Lou. "Really."

Effie was absolutely silent. Tessa smiled.

Her grandparents were the best.

. . .

"This toast!" exclaimed Ned. "It's the best! What kind is it?" Chewing loudly, he started on his third piece.

"Whole wheat," said Mrs. Gneiss. She sipped her tea. "I thought you hated whole wheat."

"If *you* made it, Mom, it's the best toast in the world and I *love* it," said Ned. He beamed, his mouth shiny with butter. A glob of jam trembled on his chin.

Mrs. Gneiss set down her cup. My son has turned into a moron, she thought, and her head twitched, as if it were trying to shake away such a terrible idea.

"Ned's right, Mom," said Nancy. "If you made it, it has to be the best, because *you're* the best!" She spoke slowly and distinctly, as if her mother were three years old and she were a nursery school teacher.

My daughter is now a moron too! thought Mrs. Gneiss, and her head twitched again.

"Is something wrong, Mom?" Nancy looked at her with concern.

"Don't you feel well?" asked Ned.

"I'm fine," lied Mrs. Gneiss. "Just fine."

# chapter 13

"**Y**ikes! We're late!" said Tod. According to Nigel's giant Rolex, the twins had seven minutes to get to school. It usually took them twelve to fourteen on their bikes.

Tessa grabbed her pack. "We better go," she said.

"Want a lift?" asked Nigel, getting up. " 'S teatime in London. Might 's well drive you."

"Cool," said Tod. He and Tessa put their bikes in the back of the Humvee and climbed into the front seat next to him.

"What does teatime in London have to do with driving us to school?" asked Tessa, who liked to know the reason for everything.

"Thought I'd try my London agent. On the car phone," said Nigel. Turning onto the road from the driveway, he picked up the phone and began to dial.

Tod and Tessa checked their seat belts. Nigel steered expertly while he was dialing, but he was driving very fast.

Wait till the kids see us in this car, thought Tod.

Dropped off by a rock star, thought Tessa.

"Don't get it!" said Nigel, slamming the car phone back into its cradle. "Nobody's taking my bleeping calls!"

"I wonder—" Tessa murmured. She was beginning to suspect the reason for Nigel's phone troubles.

"What?" asked Tod.

"Nothing."

"Better drop you off here," said Nigel. "Okay?" He pulled up at the big oak tree where Tod and Tessa parted company when they biked to school. It was about half a block from the building.

"Fine, but why?" asked Tessa.

"Problem with being . . . well known," said Nigel. "Folks get worked up when they see me. Don't want to cause a stir."

*Beep beep*, said Effie from inside Tessa's pack.

"We're still pretty late," said Tod, who wanted everybody to see him climbing out of Nigel's Hummer.

*Beep beep.*

"Oh, all right," said Nigel, adjusting his sunglasses and running his fingers through his hair. "Hate to be recognized, though."

*Beep BEEP!*

"Oh, no! Look who's out front," said Tod as they pulled up.

"Ew." Tessa's nose wrinkled. Ned and Nancy Gneiss were planted at the entrance to school, waving and smiling at them.

"Hi, Tod," said Nancy as soon as he climbed out of the Humvee. "Would you like to carry my books?"

"I would, but I, uh, sprained my wrist doing push-ups," said Tod.

*Beep beep*, said Effie.

"Cool car!" said Ned. "Who's that colorful old dude? Your grandpop?" Nigel sat in the driver's seat with the Humvee idling, his gaze on the middle distance. He looked as if he was thinking something very important—or waiting to be noticed.

Before Tod could reply to Ned, Nancy said, "You're hurt? Poor *thing*! Then I'll carry *your* books!" She snatched them away with frightening speed.

Like a cobra striking, thought Tessa, who had watched many nature documentaries. Her brother stood there with his mouth open, too stunned to protest.

"I'll help too," announced Ned, taking a few of Tod's books from Nancy.

"Uh . . . no!" said Tod. But they were inside the building already. He had no choice but to follow.

"See you," said Tessa, struggling to keep a straight face. Then she turned to wave goodbye to Nigel, who was still waiting for somebody to recognize him.

Hmmm, thought Tessa. What if . . .

Just then Watson walked up to the Humvee and tapped on the windshield. "Can't park here, buddy," he said. "Sorry."

Nigel stared at him. Then, looking very gloomy, he drove off.

The bell rang. Tessa and Watson hurried into school. "Cool car," said Watson, indicating the Humvee as it sped away.

"Did you notice who was driving?" asked Tessa. This would be a real test of her theory—Watson was very celebrity-conscious. And he'd actually been with Nigel at the mall, at least for a while.

The guard shrugged. "Not really," he said. "Just some guy."

"That's it!" said Tessa.

"What? What are you talking about?" asked Watson.

"Nothing," said Tessa. "I have to get to first period."

*Beep beep.*

Tessa raced to her locker. "No classes for you today," she whispered to Effie, parking the e-pet behind some books. "I'm putting you on a diet."

# chapter 14

As soon as classes were over, Tessa hurried to her locker. "I'll bet that Fame Ban stuff is doing something weird to Nigel," she confided in Effie. "We should go to the mall and talk to Jack." She decided to wait for Tod, who usually showed up at the lockers soon after she did.

A minute later she saw him. But he was headed in the wrong direction—toward the library—with Nancy.

"Leapin' lima beans!" whispered Tessa. "She's got him." Not only that, she was carrying his books! Had Nancy roped Tod into a study date after all? He looked as if he'd lost the will to live.

"I won't bother him right now," Tessa said to Effie. "He won't mind if I go to the mall without him."

*Beep!* said Effie. Nevertheless, Tessa biked away by

herself. She was close to the mall when she thought of something so terrible that she nearly rode her bike into a tree.

What if Tod fell for Nancy Gneiss? Ugh! She thought. How gross would that be? She picked up speed. She'd left school with one problem for Jack.

Now she had two.

"Hi there! Where's your brother?" asked Watson, who was standing at the entrance, near the revolving doors. He put on his guard's cap and adjusted his brown ponytail—getting ready for work, Tessa realized.

"Tod? He's . . . studying," said Tessa.

"Well, when you see him, tell him I have some great new stuff for my routine," said Watson as they walked inside together. "Livestock jokes—they're great! Okay?"

"Sure," said Tessa. She would never understand why her normally sensible brother found Watson funny. Even more baffling was that Tod helped Watson rehearse sometimes.

"I need his help before my next gig," said the guard.

"Another security job?" she asked, inching toward the escalator.

"No! A real gig, performing!" said Watson. "I'm the opening act at the Middle County Livestock Fair!"

"Wow," said Tessa politely. "That's soon."

"Day after tomorrow," said Watson. "I'm psyched!"

She stepped onto the escalator.

"Don't forget to tell Tod!" called Watson.

"I won't," she called back.

As usual, Level 3 was less crowded than the other floors. There were still some vacancies up here and one or two unfinished stores, as if this level were a little less desirable than the others.

Tessa wondered if she'd be able to get to Jack's without Tod. We held hands and walked backward, she thought. How hard can that be?

Turning, she took a step back. Nothing happened. Feeling very silly, she tried clasping her hands before she took another step. It worked.

The red sign appeared instantly, flashing its message on and off:

GEMINI JACK'S U RENT ALL
Be First in the Universe!

# chapter 15

*B*ong!

"Tessa? Here alone?" asked Jack, surprised.

"Yes," she said. "Tod was . . . detained."

"Imprisoned?" The voice was sharp and belonged to a woman who appeared very suddenly behind the counter next to Jack. Like Jack, she was tall and thin and had bright eyes and too many fingers. Unlike Jack, she wore a skirt and a frown.

"Not exactly," Tessa told her.

"You remember my twin sister, Jill," said Jack. "The last time you met she was orbiting Earth in a sport utility craft."

"Oh, hi," said Tessa. "Welcome to the planet." She reached out to shake hands. But she touched nothing—her fingers simply went through Jill's hand. The empty air was chilly, too.

"Whoa!" Tessa backed away.

"Jill's not really here," Jack explained. "She's orbiting again. This is a holograph."

"Oh," said Tessa, wondering why Jill looked worried.

"Where is Tod?" asked Jack.

"He's on a study date with Nancy Gneiss," said Tessa, "which is one of the reasons I came. I have to ask you a question. When you took the Gneiss twins away, what did you do to them?"

"Simple stuff. I beamed them up, extracted a few twists of their DNA—the ones linked to Vlad the Impaler—erased their memories, and sent them home," said Jill. "We hoped the Vlad samples would help us repel the Vorons. Unfortunately, they did not."

"I heard," said Tessa sympathetically. "And I'm sorry. But, uh . . . was there anything else you did to the Gneisses? Besides take samples of their DNA?"

"Well, of course," said Jill. "I straightened it out after I took the samples."

"You straightened out their DNA? Why?"

"That is the Gemini way," said Jill solemnly. "To leave things a little better than when they were found. We always improve things if we can."

"So you improved the Gneiss twins," said Tessa.

That explained a lot. "Um . . . is there any way to reverse what you did?" she asked.

"Why on Earth would you want to do that?" Jack and Jill said together.

"I know this is going to sound weird," said Tessa, "but . . . the twins? They're too nice. They're so nice it's creepy."

Jack and Jill were staring at her quizzically.

"There's this balance here on Earth between good and evil," Tessa found herself saying. "I think what you did to the twins kind of . . . upset it."

She got ready for a loud beep, but Effie was silent. Tessa swallowed. She was just making this up. What if it were true?

"Mmm," said Jill. "It is true that every planet has its own natural balance."

Amazing! thought Tessa. "Well, what if you, uh, twisted their DNA again?" she asked. "You could beam them up to your spacecraft, the way you did last time."

Jill shook her head. "A second abduction isn't possible," she said. "We've had problems with the memory erasers."

Jack said something to Jill so quietly that his mouth hardly moved.

"Ah," said Jill. She disappeared for a moment. When she returned she had a small metal box in the palm of her many-fingered hand.

"Here are the original DNA samples," she said. "If you reinsert them, the Vlad sequence will be restored. That in turn will reverse the improvements I made, and the twins will revert to normal—creepy, as you call it. If you're sure that's what you really want," she added.

Tessa thought of Ned and his offers to share and care. She thought of Nancy's sticky-sweet smile and her new crush on Tod. She lunged for the box.

"Oops!" she muttered. She'd forgotten that Jill was actually far away.

"I'll Galaxy Express it," said Jill. "Jack should get it tomorrow. Can you pick it up then?"

"Sure," said Tessa. "Bye." Jill shimmered and disappeared.

"I'd better get home too," Tessa said to Jack. "Have to do my chores before Nigel—" Suddenly she remembered the original reason she'd come to see Jack.

"Do you remember the spray you gave to Nigel? That famous guy we brought here?"

"The celebrity?" said Jack. "Yes. I gave him Fame Ban. He wanted to be nonfamous for a short while, correct?"

Tessa nodded. "But he's still nonfamous. The stuff isn't wearing off."

"Fifteen minutes and it's gone," said Jack.

"Nobody recognizes him and nobody returns his calls," said Tessa. "Plus, he's been staying with us and playing the drums nonstop, and the noise is *so* loud!"

Jack reached under the counter. He showed Tessa a spray can covered with strange markings. "See?" he said.

"I can't read that," said Tessa.

The alien made a funny little noise, part squeak, part giggle, and for an instant his eyes disappeared. "Excuse me," he said, recovering quickly. He handed her a small flashlight.

"Try this," he said. "It's a translator."

She clicked it on and aimed it at the can. When the beam hit the letters, they rearranged themselves smoothly into English. " 'Fame Ban,' " she read, " 'Fights unwanted celebrity—' " But before she could continue, Jack took the can back.

He examined it briefly and his pearly skin turned pale gray—a sign of distress. "Oh, no!" he moaned.

"What's wrong?" asked Tessa.

"I gave him the wrong one!" said Jack.

"But it says 'Fame Ban.' "

"It is Fame Ban," said Jack. "But not the fifteen-minute kind. See?" He aimed the flashlight at the label so Tessa could read it.

"Permanent!" said Jack. "And it is my fault." He moved the can closer to her so that Tessa could see the line of very small print near the bottom.

She read it and groaned. The print said EXPIRA-TION DATE: NEVER!

# chapter 16

Tessa raced home, her mind whirling faster than her bike wheels. What if Nigel had lost his celebrity forever? Would he stay at the ranch, practicing his drumphony until everybody went nuts? And what about the Gneiss twins and their DNA? Could she and Tod really reinsert it? If they did, would the mysterious and delicate planetary balance between good and evil be restored?

So little seemed certain anymore.

Tessa was hoping she'd find Tod when she got home, but his bike wasn't in the front yard when she careened up the driveway.

Nigel was definitely around, though. He was practicing again.

"How can you stand it?" Tessa asked Lou, who was once again pushing his mower around the lawn.

He glanced up at her and smiled. "Sure is," he said cheerfully. Tessa saw that he was wearing earplugs.

The din was nearly as bad in the kitchen, rattling the pots and pans, shaking the silverware, and setting off odd, metallic vibrations in the cooking utensils. Ronette and Shirelle were nowhere to be seen. Tessa wasn't surprised. The big, shaggy cats liked food and sleep, in that order. Ear-shattering percussion would drive them right into the woods, where they'd hunt innocent little rodents until the noise stopped—if it ever did.

Lulu seemed serene, however. She was taking a tray of cookies out of the oven as Tessa came in.

"How can you stand that racket?" asked Tessa.

"Of course it is, honey," Lulu replied, pouring Tessa a glass of milk. Tessa saw that Lulu was wearing earplugs too.

Tessa chewed on a peanut meringue cookie and tried not to flinch as Nigel's drumming got faster and louder. Earplugs began to seem like a good idea.

"How can you stand that racket?" asked Tod as he walked in. Lulu smiled at him placidly.

"Of course, pumpkin," she said. "Have a cookie."

Tessa rolled her eyes at her twin. She finished her cookie and cocked a thumb in the direction of the stairs, the twins' signal for "Let's talk now."

Two seconds later he joined her in her room.

"Ugh, that noise," said Tessa. She closed the windows and stuffed pillows against them. Tod pulled the curtains. Tessa shut the door, then flung herself onto her bed.

Nigel's drumming was now a distant roar, like a waterfall.

"So tell me," Tessa said. "How was your date with Never Gneiss?"

"You mean Nancy?" said Tod. "We're going steady."

"What?"

"Just kidding," said Tod. "I do have to study with her, though. She got Ms. Loam to make us partners on the rain forest report."

"Bummer!"

"She's already figured out how to research it, she's put together an outline, and she says she'll do the typing. We'll probably get an A." Tod shook his head. "She's pretty darn organized."

Humph! thought Tessa. Organization was not on her list of Top Ten Personal Strong Points. "I have news too," she said. "Good and bad."

"Bad first," said Tod.

Tessa told him about Jack's mistake with the Fame Ban, and what the label said.

" 'Permanent'? 'Expiration date: *never*'? That is bad news," said Tod. "I wonder if Nigel's figured it out yet."

"If he hasn't, he will," said Tessa. "It's been days since anybody's recognized him or asked for his autograph. Or returned his calls."

"So of course he can't reach his agents," said Tod. "He must be pretty unhappy."

An especially loud drumroll, ending with a violent crash, came from the barn.

"Make that very unhappy," said Tessa.

"There has to be an antidote," said Tod.

"Jack promised he'd think of something," said Tessa. "He's never let us down."

Tod looked doubtful. "What's the good news?"

"Personality makeover for Ned and Nancy."

"You mean—"

"Jill's sending it."

"Something to change them back? So they'll be mean again?" Tod looked ecstatic, then uncertain. "Do you think it's okay?" he asked. "I mean, there are enough bad people in the world already."

"What if there used to be just the right number," said Tessa, "and by changing the Gneiss twins, Jack upset the balance of good and evil?"

Tod stared at her. "The balance of good and evil?"

he echoed. This was not a topic that normally interested his sister.

"Maybe if they're changed back we'll be doing the universe a favor. Something that's horrible now might get better . . . Twist and Shout, for example."

"The goats?"

Tessa nodded. "They got vicious just when Jill took the Gneiss twins' DNA. What if the two things are linked?"

Tod rolled his eyes.

"Anything is possible," said Tessa, who really did believe it. Then she smiled. "No matter what else happens," she said, "Nancy will stop loving you—"

"Don't even say it!" Tod's voice cracked with desperation. He grabbed a pillow and wrapped it around his head, covering his ears. "Let's just do it!" he moaned.

"We can get it at Jack's tomorrow," said Tessa.

But Tod couldn't hear her.

# chapter 17

The drumming finally stopped at suppertime.

Good, thought Tod.

Fantastic! thought Tessa.

"Not bothering anybody," said Nigel. "Am I?"

"Not at all," said Lou and Lulu together.

*Beep beep,* called Effie from the stairway.

"Super!" Nigel said, joining them at the table. "Decided I'm ready."

"Ready?" asked Lou.

"Ready to play the whole thing," said Nigel. "The entire Drummerdämmerung! Big finale—clash of the cymbals—should come at dawn."

"Cymbals at sunrise," said Lou. "My, my."

"How . . . nice," said Lulu.

*Beep beep,* said Effie.

Tod and Tessa looked at each other.

I have lost my appetite, said Tod's expression.

So have I, said Tessa's.

The drums started right after supper and got louder and louder as the twins did their homework. At nine, just as they were getting ready for bed, the drums stopped.

"What a relief!" exclaimed Tessa as she turned off her light.

Tod, ever cautious, put a pillow over his head.

But the drums never started up again. The ranch was quiet all night long, and the twins got their first full night of sleep in days.

They came down to breakfast feeling cheerful and rested. Lulu hummed as she made pancakes. Lou harmonized while he squeezed the orange juice.

Only Nigel was less than bright-eyed. He showed up just as everybody was finishing, mumbled an apology, and put his cell phone next to his plate. "Know you hate these things," he said to Lulu. "Still, can't miss my agent's call."

"You still haven't heard from her?" asked Lulu.

"Must be stuck in meetings," said Nigel. He bit into a pancake. "Hope I didn't keep you up last night," he said. "Played the drumphony all the way through. At concert volume."

"You did?" said Lou.

"We must have slept through it," said Lulu. "Is that possible?"

Nigel shrugged. "Dunno," he said. "But I did start late. Practiced a bit, then took a nap. Had the weirdest dream—straight out of an old sci-fi flick."

"Flying saucers?" asked Lou. "Aliens?"

"That's right," said Nigel. He looked at his Rolex and stood. "Tell you about it later. Want to drive the kids to school."

"Cool," said Tod, who loved riding in the Humvee.

Tessa wondered why Nigel wanted to give them a lift. She found out as soon as they were on the highway.

"Been thinking," said Nigel, raising his voice over the sound of a thousand bongos. "This not having my calls returned? Could be a glitch with my phone. The trees? The livestock? Might be blocking my incoming."

"Could be," said Tod.

*Beep beep*, said Effie.

"Either that or they're avoiding me," said Nigel.

"People are weird," said Tessa politely. She threw her jacket over her pack to muffle Effie's beep, but Effie remained quiet.

"Well, here we are," said Nigel as he pulled up to the school. "Jump out quick before I get mobbed."

Poor guy, thought Tessa. How long will he keep pretending that everything's okay? She pulled her bike out of the Humvee, feeling guilty because she knew what the problem was but couldn't tell Nigel.

"That dream you had?" Tod asked Nigel. "What was it like?"

"Quite nice, actually," said Nigel. "Spacecraft in orbit. Beautiful alien woman, said she was a fan. Asked me to play my drumphony for her. So I did."

"Did she like it?" asked Tessa.

"Loved it," said Nigel.

*Beep beep!* said Effie.

## chapter 18

Poor guy, thought Tod. Hope Jack's got the Fame Ban antidote. But as soon as the Humvee pulled away, Tod stopped feeling sorry for Nigel and started feeling sorry for himself.

All it took was the sugary sound of Nancy's voice, calling out to him from down the hall.

"Tod! Oh, Tod-ee!"

Tod-ee? Tod groaned, but she was charging at him like a bull at a red flag.

"Tod!" she gasped. "I have a note for you!"

"A note? Sorry, but I, uh . . ." Tod quelled a violent urge to run. Kids were watching! He heard some giggles—a bunch of fifth-grade girls was monitoring Nancy's approach—and felt his ears turn red.

Tod had once heard Lulu say that she was a private person, and now he understood what she'd meant.

Privacy! he thought with yearning. At least his family (including Tessa, usually) and his friends knew when to leave him alone. They got that he was quiet—what Lulu called "retiring"—and that he didn't like to draw attention to himself. Most of the time he actually liked being ignored, so that he could watch the world around him and think his own thoughts.

But that definitely wasn't happening now, and it was most unpleasant.

"Here," said Nancy, placing an envelope firmly in his hand. "It's specially for you. Don't let anyone else read it, okay?" She blew him a kiss and ran off.

Tod tried not to think about the note in science class, but everything Mr. Brock said about the social habits of insects reminded him of Nancy. She was *predatory*! And she had selected *him*!

As proof, there was her note, in a pink envelope with little flowers all over it. She had written TOD in big letters on the front, surrounding his name with a huge, neatly drawn heart.

Ack! thought Tod. Grisly! He folded the envelope over and over until it was no bigger than a stick of gum and put it in his pocket, wishing it would disappear.

Wishing *she* would disappear.

But Nancy appeared everywhere—in the stairwell, across the room in history class, even at the water fountain while he was getting a drink.

"Did you read it yet?" she whispered at the fountain, which made him choke and forced water out his nose. Coughing, he shook his head and ran away. I should just toss it, he thought miserably.

But he couldn't.

Finally he was in English, his last class of the day. He looked up from his notebook to see Kathy Gardiner staring at him.

Oh, no! he thought. Another girl is paying attention to me! What's happening? He looked at her. She smiled, and his stomach turned over.

"What?" he blurted out.

"What do you mean, what?" she asked, her smile fading.

"Uh, why are you staring at me?" Please don't have a crush on me, he thought. Please! I can't take it!

"Actually," she said, "you have ketchup on your nose, and I was trying to figure out a nice way to tell you. But never mind."

"Oh," said Tod.

When the bell finally rang, he ran for the bike rack. Tessa got there just as he did.

"Where's your girlfriend?" she asked.

"Very funny," said Tod. "Can we please just get out of here before—" A familiar voice interrupted him and he shuddered.

"Tod! Tod-ee! Where are you?"

He pedaled away so fast his tires left skid marks.

# chapter 19

*C*ycling frantically, Tod led them to the mall in just under fifteen minutes.

"Yow!" exclaimed Tessa as they parked their bikes. "I think we set a new record!" Panting, she swiped at the sweat on her forehead and resisted the temptation to tease her brother. She knew why he'd raced here.

Can't blame him, she thought. I'd be in a hurry too if Nancy were after me.

"We can't stay too long," he said. "We have to help Lou with the goats, remember?" The twins had promised to groom Twist and Shout for the livestock show, which was the following day.

"Brushing, braiding, and tie-dyed bows," said Tessa grimly. "I can hardly wait." She had made up her mind to wear padding—soccer guards, pillows, her down parka—while she worked. Enough was enough.

"Here we are," said Tod as they reached Level 3. As usual it was quieter than the other floors.

The twins whirled around and clasped hands, almost as if they were square dancing. Then they took two steps backward in unison.

The neon sign appeared instantly, flashing on and then off:

## GEMINI JACK'S U RENT ALL
### Be First in the Universe!

"Look," said Tod as they approached. "He's got a customer. Weird." Jack was almost always alone in his shop.

"She's not a customer," said Tessa. "She's his sister, and she's not really there."

"What do you mean, not there?" said Tod. "She's right in front of us." Sometimes Tessa could be annoyingly illogical.

"You'll see," she said.

*Bong!*

"Hello, Earth twins," said Jack. "You've met my sister, Jill."

"Greetings," said Jill, extending her hand.

Tod reached out to shake it, and his hand went right through hers. He felt a chill, like the cold mist that came out of Lulu's freezer on a hot day.

"Whoa!" he said, startled. Jack made an odd squeaking sound and for a moment his eyes disappeared.

"She's transmitting holographically from her sport utility craft," Tessa explained.

"Oh," said Tod. Why are girls always right? he wondered, hoping Tessa hadn't noticed his reaction to Jill.

Luckily her mind was on other things. "Did you beam Nigel up to your spacecraft last night?" she asked Jill.

"I did," said Jill. "Jack asked me to help, and I wanted to make sure he'd used the wrong Fame Ban."

"And?"

"He did."

"You mean Nigel will never be a celebrity again, ever?"

"The only antidote to Fame Ban is on Gemini. It's so highly volatile that it can't be transported. Interstellar flight destroys it."

"Poor Nigel!" said Tessa. "This will break his heart." Then she imagined life at the ranch with

Nigel and quaked. I don't want to wear earplugs! she thought. I'm too young!

Jack looked confused. "When your friend was here, he said he disliked being a celebrity."

"That's just something celebrities say," said Tessa. "They actually dislike *not* being famous."

"Are you sure the Fame Ban doesn't just wear off?" asked Tod.

Jack spread his many fingers in a gesture of hopelessness. " 'Expiration date: never,' " he said.

"Wait! What if he went to Gemini?" said Tessa. "You could give him the antidote there."

"It is a long trip," said Jack. "And most humans could not tolerate our planets' atmospheres, which flash with bright lights and emit a constant electronic crackle."

"He's a rock star," said Tod. "That's perfect for him."

"Please!" begged Tessa. "You promised."

Jack and Jill looked at each other and engaged in a very rapid silent dialogue.

"Actually, we are looking into it," Jack said finally.

"But don't get your hopes up just yet," cautioned Jill. "There are arrangements to be made, contracts to be negotiated, permissions, warranties . . ."

"Meanwhile," said Jack, opening his many-fingered

hand to reveal a tiny metallic box, "here is the original DNA we extracted from the Gneiss twins."

Tod felt a rush of hope and joy. "And it'll really change them back?" he asked.

"Just as before," said Jill. "You simply have to insert it."

"Insert it?" echoed the twins.

"Yes," said Jack. "For Ned, it goes right here." He pointed at the smooth featureless side of his head. "On humans there is an opening."

"His ear? We have to stick it in his ear?" said Tessa.

"For Ned," repeated Jack.

"And . . . for Nancy?" asked Tod.

"For Nancy, the opening is here," said Jill, pointing to her nose.

"*What?* It goes in her nose?" Tod was practically screaming.

"You have a problem with that?" asked Jill.

"We—we don't want to get that close," he managed to say.

"Well, all right," said Jill. She said something to Jack and he reached for the box.

"Wait!" said Tessa. "We'll figure out a way to do it. Won't we, Tod?" She glared at him.

He swallowed. I wanted a get-rid-of-Nancy gadget, he thought. And here it is. "Yes," he said.

Tessa put the box into her pack.

"About your problem?" Tod said to Jack and Jill. "I've been thinking about it—"

"You have?" Tessa felt guilty. She had been so caught up in her own problems that she'd forgotten Jack and Jill's request for help.

"You wanted something so annoying that it would drive the Vorons away forever, right?" asked Tod.

"That is correct," said Jill. "I have been working on the problem also," she said. "And I think I have found a solution, though there are arrangements to be made."

"But I *have* the solution," said Tod. "Buy Twist and Shout—my grandfather's goats."

"Goats?" said Jill.

"Goats are annoying?" asked Jack.

"Very," said Tessa, with complete conviction. "If you need proof, I can show you—"

A shout came from the corridor, then another.

"What's going on out there?" asked Jack.

There were more shouts, and now they could see people hurrying to the escalator. Tod opened the door.

"Call Security!" somebody yelled from Level 2. "And lock up the houseplants!"

# chapter 20

**F**ar away. Far away. That was where they had to go. They both knew it, and they acted together, chewing through their halters and ropes, pushing through the opening in the barn door, and then running, running, running.

Away from the noise. Away from the bashing and the clanging and the evil Two Legs who would not stop tormenting them.

Twist wanted to butt him on the way out of the barn, but Shout let him know that either they would run without stopping or she would commit goat suicide, so they kept going.

There was nobody outside, not that any Two Legs could have caught them, but still, it saved them the trouble of performing one of their many evasion routines, which had been getting downright boring.

And it felt so good to be out of there, in the fragrant green fields, then scampering down the dirt road scaring all the cars.

But the best part, Twist thought later, was realizing how hungry they were once they got inside the Giant Barn and then making the soul-stirring discovery that every single thing in the Giant Barn was edible. Crunchy things. Soft things. Chewy things. Hairy things. All they had to do was chase away the Two Legs, which was so ridiculously easy, and then eat to their hearts' content.

Twist's belly was full. He was at peace. He communicated these thoughts to Shout with a contented *Baaa!*

The best part, thought Shout, was when the Two Legs with the soft, eager voice came and told them jokes after they ate. There is nothing like a good laugh to aid goatly digestion, but how many Two Legs know this important fact and act on it? All too few.

Shout communicated these thoughts to Twist with a melodious *Baaa!* and then they both fell asleep.

Before she fell asleep that night Tessa imagined being interviewed by an eager reporter about the afternoon's emergency at the mall.

"Exciting, yes," she would say. "Exciting but

unpleasant. I guess you've never chased goats through a mall," she would add, as if she were referring to an elite, dangerous sport—X-treme Goat Herding. The reporter, eyes gleaming with admiration, would admit that she'd never had the opportunity, and Tessa would nod knowingly. Then Tessa would mention, very casually, that she knew Watson.

"Is that so!" the reporter would exclaim. Then Tessa would tell her exactly how it happened that Watson—the guard who walked the halls of Middle Valley Middle School telling cringe-worthy jokes—Watson, with a little help from Tessa and her brother, Tod, had averted catastrophe that afternoon. How Watson had prevented a riot and subdued two berserk Patagonians by doing something completely unexpected and amazing, though it made perfect sense when you thought about it . . .

As he dropped off to sleep that night, Tod thought about what he'd tell his friends at school the next day about the Goat Incident at the Mall.

He'd describe the shoppers, some alarmed, some—like the children—bouncing with excitement. He'd mention the weird trail he and Tessa had followed: half-chewed plastic packages of white athletic socks; toppled potted palms with mangled leaves; the capsized snack cart; soft pretzels, some still covered with mustard; and the scattering of blue and green and pink and purple spiky wigs that led them, finally, to the fountain—and the weirdest sight of all.

For there at the fountain sat Watson, with the goats. He was perfectly calm, and so were they.

First he whispered into Twist's ear, and Twist said "Baaa!" Then he whispered into Shout's ear, and Shout said "Baaa!"

Tod had never seen anything like it.

"And get this," Tod would say to his friends. "The reason they were listening to him? He was telling them *jokes. Goat* jokes."

As the twins fell asleep, the adults sat in the kitchen talking. Actually, Lou and Lulu were talking; Nigel was brooding.

It wasn't so much what they'd said about the goats, although he refused to believe those animals had run all the way from the ranch to the mall just to get away from his drumming.

And it wasn't that his agents still hadn't returned his calls, though that rankled too. No, thought Nigel, as his friends rambled on about the livestock show the next day, and how great it was going to be with the goats so cooled out (thanks to Watson and his goat jokes) that they might even win a ribbon. It wasn't either of those things that was bringing him down so low.

It was that Lou and Lulu—old friends, music lovers, free spirits just like himself—had asked him to please stop practicing his drumphony so they could get some sleep.

It hurt.

In the mall, Jack was winding up a conversation with his twin. "If it works it will solve more than one problem," he said. "Are you sure?"

"I heard it last night," said Jill. "The whole thing, all the way through. If it doesn't work, nothing will."

"Wonderful," said Jack. "Should I make the arrangements?"

"Why not?" said Jill. "I did the hard part."

"I'll start right away," said Jack.

As soon as Jill broke contact, Jack picked up a telephone. "Hello, Operator," he said. "I need a number in London, please. And one in Hollywood."

# chapter 21

*T*he twins didn't notice that Nigel was quieter than usual the following morning. They were too busy thinking about the little metal box Jack had given them and the incredibly powerful, extremely difficult-to-insert spirals of DNA it contained.

Yet Nigel was quiet. He didn't play a loud tape or beat the steering wheel like a conga drum or even say much while he drove them to school. Which was probably why the twins actually heard the phone ring in the Humvee just as he drove away.

"Wonder who's calling him," said Tessa. "Maybe it's one of his agents."

"Hope so," said Tod. He'd been looking forward to describing yesterday's scene at the mall to his friends, but now, in the bright light of morning, he knew that before he did that, he was going to have to deal with

Nancy and her nose. It occurred to Tod that he usually had to do something—homework, or chores, or putting DNA into a horrible girl's nose—before he was allowed to have any fun. He sighed.

"I've got the DNA in my pack," said Tessa as they walked into school. "Who should go first?"

"You," said Tod.

Tessa wasn't surprised. Girls always had to do the hard stuff first.

"Nigel, dearest, how are you?"

"Clarissa? Where've you been? I've been phoning you for days!"

"Darling boy, I won't lie. I've been working on something very, very special for you, but I wanted everything in place before I called."

"Special?" asked Nigel. "What do you mean?"

"Are you sitting down?" asked Clarissa.

"Yes, I'm sitting down, I'm in the Hummer," said Nigel.

"Good. How would you like to perform the Drummerdämmerung for an audience of, oh, sixty or seventy million?" she asked.

Nigel's heart pounded like a tom-tom. "That's what you've been working on?"

"I have."

"When? And where?"

"Two days from now," said Clarissa. "Live, broadcast over the entire planet. At whatever volume you choose."

Nigel started to choke up. After a moment he asked, "As loud as I like?"

"As loud as you like."

"You're not joking, Clarissa, are you?" asked Nigel. "Because you know how much this means to me." Behind his rose-colored glasses, his eyes got misty.

"It's all arranged, dear boy, I promise. You're booked and they're waiting, so pack your bags. *Ciao, bello.*"

"Wait! Where'm I going?" asked Nigel. But Clarissa had hung up.

He smiled. The truth was, he didn't care.[10]

---

[10] Celebrity Rule *10: Celebrities will go very far to restore their celebrity, if they've lost it.

# chapter 22

GOAT WHISPERER SAVES THE DAY! said the headline, which had been clipped from the newspaper and pinned to the bulletin board on the main floor.

*Two rampaging goats broke into Middle Valley Mall today, mauling houseplants, toppling a snack cart, and lowering their horns at shoppers. In the ensuing panic, many customers hid behind counters and in rest rooms. There were no fatalities, though two cases of critical butting were reported.*

*One person whose calm may have prevented more serious damage was Alfonse "Al" Watson, a security guard and part-time entertainer whose handling of the out-of-control goats drew praise from many shaken shoppers.*

*"I was so freaked, I broke three nails!" said one emotional teenager. "Then he came and started whispering to them—the goats, I mean, not my nails—and they totally calmed down."*

"Pretty neat, huh?" said Tessa, forcing herself to stand close to Ned Gneiss, who was reading the clipping avidly.

"You bet!" said Ned. "I put it up myself. It's such an awesome story, I thought everyone should read it! Watson is so incredible, don't you think? I mean, he's funny *and* he's brave!"

"I totally agree," said Tessa.

*Beep beep*, said Effie from inside Tessa's pack.

"What was that?" asked Ned.

"Just an alien fib muncher," mumbled Tessa, taking one of the two tiny DNA spirals out of the tin.

"What?"

Tessa smiled brightly, ignoring Ned's question. "Have you heard Watson's latest joke?" she asked.

"No!" Ned beamed with anticipation. "Tell me!"

"Lean down," she said, "so I can whisper it in your ear."

A second later he straightened up, scowling. "That is so totally stupid!" he said loudly, his hands balling into fists.

Tessa's eyes widened and she smiled with delight. This only made Ned angrier.

"Get lost, you hippie creep!" he cried, backing away from her.

"Happy to," said Tessa, beaming. She was still grinning a few minutes later when she found Tod near the Horticulture Club's flower-arranging exhibit.

"It *worked*!" she announced. "Really fast, too! Now it's your turn."

"I . . . I can't!" said Tod. "I can't figure out how!"

Tessa thought for a moment. "Here's an idea," she said, whispering it to him.

Tod considered it. "Okay," he said. "I have library with her—I'll try it then."

"Tod! Tod-ee! There you are!"

Tod forced a smile and set his books down next to Nancy's on the library table. He had a plan, but he was still numb with dread.

"Did you read my note?" she whispered, standing very close to him. Her nostrils, he noticed, were pretty big. That was good.

"Uh, not yet," he said. "But I brought you something." He held out the tulip that Tessa had given him. It was a little bedraggled, but Nancy didn't seem to mind.

"A flower! Oh, that is *so sweet!*" she crooned.

"You have to smell it," said Tod. Nancy closed her eyes, plunged her nose into the tulip, and took a deep breath.

An instant later, as she opened her eyes, Tod watched her face tighten, and narrow, and harden. It was a horrible, fascinating transformation.

"Get lost, nerd ball!" she spat, throwing the tulip down and grinding it into the floor with an extremely white sneaker.

"Does that mean I don't have to read this?" asked Tod, holding out her note.

She grabbed the note and tore it to pieces, which fell to the library floor like pink snow.

"I guess not," said Tod, grinning.

"Mr. Bradshaw!" called Nancy, her voice like a rusty chainsaw. "Tod Gibson is bothering me! He won't let me study! And I have a report to do!"

"Tod?" called Mr. Bradshaw from his desk. "Come here, please!"

"Bye, Nancy," said Tod.

Her look of disgust was wonderful to see.

# chapter 23

"**D**id it work?" Tessa asked her twin when they met after school.

"Sure did," he said. "So well that Nancy reported me for stealing the tulip. I had to apologize to the Horticulture Club and promise to plant bulbs with them in the fall."

"Gee," said Tessa.

"It was worth it," said Tod. "Anything's worth it."

"Want to go to the mall to thank Jack and Jill?" asked Tessa. "It's the least we can do."

"Least we can do? What do you mean?" Tod asked as they climbed onto their bikes.

"We haven't solved their problem, remember?"

"Oh!" Tessa's reminder took Tod from bliss to chagrin in three seconds. "Sure, let's go," he said, leading the way.

But when they got to Level 3 and went through their Jack-finding routine, Gemini Jack's U Rent All didn't appear. They tried three times, but they just couldn't find it.

Tessa hadn't expected this disappointment, and it was sharp and painful. She wanted to see Jack and Jill very badly—to thank them for restoring the Gneiss twins, and to work on the Voron problem. She and Tod owed them that.

We owe them big-time, she thought. Look what they did for us!

"What a bummer," said Tod. He looked up and down the corridor again, hoping desperately that Gemini Jack's would appear.

But it didn't.

"Do you think he's gone? Wonder why he didn't say goodbye," said Tod.

Tessa was wondering the same thing. Jack was very polite, after all. Still, he was nowhere in sight. "Guess we should go," she said, and they turned in the direction of the escalator.

A tiny red flash near the escalator—coming from something on the floor—caught Tessa's eye. "Is that a doll?" she asked. Whatever it was flashed again.

"Don't know," said Tod listlessly.

"It is a doll!" Tessa ran past Tod and picked it up.

"Holy Moly!" she cried. "This is amazing! It looks just like Jack!"

"What?" Tod came closer. "It's an action figure," he told his sister, "not a doll." Girls! he thought.

Then he looked again. It was pretty amazing—a ten-inch replica of Jack, with movable joints, pearly skin, and bright little eyes. Which, Tod saw now, were blinking. Every time they did, there was a tiny red flash.

"Wow," he said. I bet they left this for us, he thought.

"They left this for us, I'm positive," said Tessa. "And look, the eyes are blinking!"

Tod had read enough science fiction to know what they'd found.

"It's an interplanetary communication device," he told Tessa. "Let me see it."

Tessa handed it over. Tod tried unscrewing the head, but it didn't come off. He felt its surface for buttons, but there weren't any. He shook it. Nothing happened. But the eyes kept blinking.

"Hmm," said Tod. He passed a hand in front of the figure's face.

Writing—very small red letters—scrolled across his palm. His mouth dropped open. "They're sending us a message," he said.

"Aah!" A gasp of surprise came from Tessa.

"Shhh!" cautioned Tod. Then they both read the message.

> T & T:
> SORRY TO LEAVE WITHOUT SAYING GOODBYE.
> FAREWELL AND THANKS.
> WE'LL LET YOU KNOW HOW IT GOES.
> J & J & N

"That's from Jack and Jill for sure," said Tessa.

"N?" said Tod. "Who's N?"

"I think I know," said Tessa. As they biked home, she explained her theory to Tod.

"No way," he declared as they dropped their bikes in the front yard. "You're crazy."

The barn door opened and Lou emerged, leading Twist and Shout. They looked clean and silky—as brushed, powdered, polished, and buffed as champion poodles. Even more striking was their calm.

Then Tod realized that the ranch was quiet, even though Nigel's Humvee was parked in front. That was unusual too.

Lou loaded the goats into his truck. "We have to leave now," he called. "You kids ride with Lulu."

"The livestock show!" The twins looked at each other. They had forgotten all about it.

"Is Nigel coming?" called Tod.

Lou shook his head. "Nigel's gone."

"Gone?" squeaked Tod.

Tessa grinned. "Now who's crazy?" she whispered. She loved being right.

Lulu came outside wearing a flowered dress and a big straw hat. "Nigel's agent called this morning," she said. "Right after he took you to school."

"I thought I heard the phone ring in the Humvee!" said Tessa.

"Great news," said Lulu. "He's finally going to perform his Drummer . . . his drumphony, or whatever it's called."

"I'm splitting, you guys!" called Lou from his truck. "Catch you later!"

"See you at the show!" called Lulu. She climbed into the Humvee, fastened her seat belt, and started the engine. There was a deafening boom—drum music—which she quickly turned off.

"Did Nigel say . . . where he was going?" asked Tessa once they were inside.

Lulu shook her head. "He told Lou, but of course Lou forgot. All he can think about is those silly goats." She maneuvered the gigantic SUV down the driveway and onto the road. "Still, Nigel was ecstatic when he left. He kept saying the gig was 'an out-of-this-world opportunity.' "

# chapter 24

"**I** thought the best part was Watson," said Tod late that night. He yawned. He and Tessa were comparing notes on the livestock show, talking through the curtain between their rooms. "That joke about Planet of the Goats cracked me up."

"I thought the best part was seeing Grandpa Lou when Twist and Shout won," said Tessa. "He just couldn't get over how well-behaved they were." She yawned. "But it was great when that Internet guy—Bob Fences?—the gazillionaire?—bought them, too."

"And flew them out of the fair in his chopper," said Tod.

"Good riddance," murmured Tessa, her eyes closing. The ranch, now that Nigel was gone, was very quiet. She yawned again. "You know what?"

"What?"

"I don't miss the drums, but I miss Nigel."

"Me too," said Tod.

"The worst part was being paged," said Mrs. Gneiss. "Everybody at the fair heard us being called to the security office."

"The worst part was paying that popcorn vendor for his damages," said Mr. Gneiss. "How those two managed to get bloodred dye into his machine is beyond me."

"The security guard is talking about filing a personal injury suit against Nancy," said Mrs. Gneiss. "He says she inflicted grievous bodily harm."

"What? How?"

"With her fingernails. They're very sharp and pointy. You know. The way they used to be," said Mrs. Gneiss. "Before."

There was a brief silence in the kitchen.

"It was only a flesh wound," she added.

"Well, then," said Mr. Gneiss. "No harm done." He sipped his tea.

A heavy thud came from upstairs, followed by an angry shout, a crash, a shriek, and the sound of doors slamming. The noises were so loud they produced a network of very faint cracks in the kitchen ceiling, yet all Mr. Gneiss said was, "I think I'll have a little more tea, Mirjana."

"What a good idea," she said, pouring for both of them.

The next day after school, Tod and Tessa hurried upstairs to check on the action figure, now called Little Jack, who was stationed on Tod's bureau.

His eyes were blinking.

"A message!" said Tessa, holding out her palm to reflect the scrolling red letters.

BAD NEWS.
THE VORONS LOVE NIGEL.
THEY ARE ARRIVING IN GREATER NUMBERS THAN EVER BEFORE.
J & J

"Oh, no!" said Tessa. "It backfired! That's terrible!"

"Sure is," said Tod, looking pained.

But they both knew there was nothing they could do.

The next day Little Jack's eyes were blinking again. Tod held out his palm for the message.

GOOD NEWS.

THE VORONS LOVE NIGEL SO MUCH THEY'VE TAKEN HIM

TO THEIR OWN PLANET. GEMINI IS PEACEFUL AT LAST.

THANK YOU, T & T.

J & J

"Wow. That's a relief," said Tod.

"I'll say," agreed Tessa. "I just hope Nigel is happy."

He was, according to the postcard that arrived the next day.

It was addressed to Lou and Lulu and Tod and Tessa, and at first everybody thought it was from the twins' parents, but the picture on the card was like no place on Earth. It showed a brightly lit city with soaring glass towers and two moons in the sky, one pink and one blue.

The card itself was creased and battered. Its edges were singed, as if it had come too close to a star or two before landing in Lou and Lulu's old red mailbox.

"Wow, look at this," said Lou. The handwriting was a jagged purple scrawl.

"Read it, honey," said Lulu.

" 'Having a wonderful time. Wish you were here,' " he read.

"Is that all?" asked Tessa, recognizing Nigel's handwriting.

★ 114 ★

"There's more," said Lou. "Listen to this: 'Hey, Lulu, remember when you told me that people won't sit still for a long drum solo? Well, people won't, but the Vorons will! Love to all, Nigel.' "

"Vorons?" said Lulu. "What's that, a rock group?"

"Could be," said Tod and Tessa together.

*Beep beep,* said Effie.

# Watson's Goat Jokes

Two goats are in a field, munching grass. It's a beautiful, sunny day. Suddenly one turns to the other and says, "Moo!"

"What?" says the other goat, startled.

"It's always good to know a second language," says the first goat.

A man and a goat get married and have a child. One day a salesman knocks on the front door of their house and the child peeks out.

"Hi there," says the salesman. "Is your mother at home?"

The child lowers its head slightly and calls, "*Maaaaa! Maaaaaa!*"

A man is driving along the highway with a carful of goats. There are goats in the front seat, goats in the backseat, and goats hanging out the windows.

A state trooper pulls the man over.

"Just what do you think you're doing?" he demands.

"Taking these goats for a ride," says the man.

"Taking them for a ride!" exclaims the trooper. "Take them to the zoo!" And he drives off.

The next day, the trooper sees the same man with the same carful of goats. Once again he pulls him over.

"I thought I told you to take these goats to the zoo!" he says.

"I did," says the man. "And we had so much fun that today I'm taking them to the movies."

# ABOUT THE AUTHORS

Stephanie Spinner is the coauthor, with Jonathan Etra, of *Aliens for Breakfast*, winner of the Texas Bluebonnet Award, and its companions, *Aliens for Lunch* and *Aliens for Dinner*. She lives in New York City.

Terry Bisson's *Bears Discover Fire* won both the Hugo and Nebula awards, science fiction's highest honors. His *Pirates of the Universe* was a *New York Times* Notable Book of 1996. He too lives in New York City.